Onions Can Make a Grown Man Cry

AND

Other Short Stories

by Nancy Lee Mauer

DORRANCE
PUBLISHING CO
EST. 1920
PITTSBURGH, PENNSYLVANIA 15238

Dorrance Publishing Co
585 Alpha Drive
Pittsburgh, PA 15238
Visit our website at www.dorrancebookstore.com

ISBN: 979-8-88925-404-1
eISBN: 979-8-88925-904-6

NANCY LEE MAUER AND HER HUSBAND, MATT OPER-
ATED A DAIRY FARM IN MASON COUNTY IN NORTHERN
MICHIGAN UNTIL RECENTLY. He died September 27, 2022, at
the age of ninety-three and a half. Nancy is the age of eighty-nine.
Being very active until the end, Matt took care of most of the work
himself until it was time to turn the farm over to the youngest son.
Nancy has a certain amount of cow knowledge from living all of these
years on the farm. The Mauers had been married nearly sixty-seven
years. They had eleven children, 31 grandchildren, 23 great grandchildren, and 7 great-great grandchildren.

MAD COW DISEASE

In early June, Susie waltzed up to her dad, Matt Farmer, while he was milking cows.

"Dad, can I take some cows to the fair?"

Matt Farmer removed the milker from the cow he was milking. He held the milker in his left hand. He lifted his red baseball cap and scratched his head with his right hand.

"I dunno. It's a lot of work getting a cow ready for the fair. I won't have time to help you. I'm too busy making hay, cultivating corn, spraying for weeds, and fertilizing the hay fields. You'll have to take them out and teach them to lead."

"I know, Dad. I'm sixteen, almost seventeen. I can do it."

Matt snorted. "You won't be seventeen for eight more months." He attached the milker to the next cow. "Which cow did you want to take?"

Susie scuffed her foot in the sawdust on the floor behind the cows.

Matt knew she was working up to something.

Finally, she said, "Actually, I want to take three cows."

A worried look crossed Matt's face. He thought, *Oh, oh. I smell trouble.* He asked his daughter, "Which three cows?"

After hemming and hawing, she admitted. "I want to take Hazel, Henrietta, and Hildegarde."

"Those three troublemakers? You'd have your hands full with those three. Every time something goes wrong around here, those three are involved."

"I can handle them, Dad. I used to lead them when they were calves. In fact, I'm sure I took all three of them to the fair when they were babies. Please, Dad, after I take them out and lead them a few times, they'll be okay."

"What about milking them at the fair? I won't be able to help you. I'll be milking the herd here at home."

"Don't worry, Dad. You can show me how. I'm sure some of the guys will help me. I'll manage."

Matt Farmer could never refuse his daughter anything she asked for. She wasn't really spoiled, just loved by both her parents, but especially her father. He was an old softy, and she knew it.

"Get them out and practice with them every day; prove to me you can handle them, then I'll let you take them."

Maybe Matt couldn't help her every day, but he'd be in stands at the fairgrounds on show day. No amount of hay to bale would keep him away.

Susie danced a little jig. "Thanks, Dad."

She ran toward her mother who was feeding calves their milk.

"Mom, Dad said I can take Hazel, Henrietta, and Hildegarde to the fair." She clapped her hands and danced some more.

Her mother laughed as she measured milk replacer into warm water. "Do you really think you can handle those three troublemakers?"

"Sure, I can. I led them when they were babies. I'll practice with them all summer. I can hardly wait." She picked up a curry comb and combed Hazel's red and white body, humming happily to herself. She sang softly, "We're going to the fair. We're going to the fair."

By the middle of August, Susie had practiced leading all three cows until they knew exactly what was expected of them. Wonder of wonders, they usually did what she wanted them to do. She gave them baths and clipped their hair. The cows were as ready as they would ever be. Matt Farmer took them to the fairgrounds in a livestock trailer pulled by his old blue Dodge pickup truck.

They found the stalls assigned to their cows, spread bales of straw so the cows had plenty of bedding. It's very important to keep the cows clean at the fair. They led the cows to the stalls and tied them in place. After they were tied in place, Susie fed them plenty of hay. Typical of a cow, Hazel reached over and ate Henrietta's hay so she could save hers for later.

Angela Leadbottom had a cow in the stall next to Susie's cows. She took some of Susie's hay and fed it to her cow. Not wanting to start a fight, Susie ignored the theft of hay.

Angela sniffed, nose in the air. "My cow can beat your cows any day."

Susie said, "I don't think so." She turned and walked away to avoid any more arguments.

Early in the morning, the day of the show, Susie milked the cows. Then she led them one by one to the washstand, shampooed them, then rinsed off the suds. While she was rinsing the last one, she was hit by a blast of cold water. She looked in the direction of the water.

Angela was at the business end of the hose. She innocently said, "Oh, did I get you wet? I was just rinsing off my cow."

Susie couldn't prove anything different, but she thought Angela sprayed her on purpose. She decided she'd have to be more careful about what was going on next time. Luckily, she hadn't changed into her good clothes yet, so no real damage was done.

During the showmanship event, Susie led Henrietta around the ring. Angela followed Susie and Henrietta with her cow. Susie kept her eye on the judge and paid no attention to Angela or any of the other contestants. Henrietta performed beautifully and the judge motioned Susie into first place.

Angela pulled a small jackknife out of her pocket and poked Henrietta in the rear. Naturally, the cow jumped and sidestepped. Susie quickly yanked on the halter, talked softly to the cow, and settled her down. The extremely nervous cow, knowing Angela stood behind her, lifted her tail and did what cows do naturally. During the act, Henrietta suddenly coughed.

Poor Angela was peppered with flying manure. She coughed, sputtered, and wailed, "Look what your cow did. You did it on purpose."

The judge said, "Young lady, you're way off base. No one can make a cow perform a bodily function. That comes naturally. Any more outbursts and you'll leave the show ring. Do you understand?"

Angela's face turned crimson. She meekly turned back to her cow, but Susie knew she hadn't seen the last of Angela Leadbottom. She was one girl who would get even one way or another.

The showmanship class ended with the judge awarding Susie and Henrietta first place. She received a trophy and a blue ribbon.

The judge said, "Even though her cow jumped, she managed to keep her under control. That's good showmanship."

After lunch, they held the show that judged the animals. First, they judged the calves. Then heifers, beginning with the youngest, on up until they got to the cows. Susie left Henrietta and Hazel in the barn while she showed Hildegarde in the Brown Swiss class.

While the barn was virtually empty, Angela furtively took a bottle of apple scented shampoo and poured it into Henrietta's water-bowl. Being a curious cow, Henrietta sniffed. Evidently, she liked the apple scent. She took a big drink. It was good for a second, then the aftertaste set in. She snorted. Bubbles flowed from her mouth and nose.

Ugh! What a horrible taste! She took another drink from her waterbowl. Bubbles foamed and poured from her mouth. She panicked, reared, and pulled back. The halter broke and she left her stall, intent on finding a clean drink of water.

Henrietta spied Angela carrying a bucket of water and made a bee-line for her.

Angela yelled, "Mad cow! Mad cow! Mama, help."

Mrs. Leadbottom heard her daughter and came running. She chorused, "Mad cow!" with her daughter. The two of them climbed over a gate so fast everyone who saw them laughed.

The enraged Mrs. Leadbottom hated being the object of laughter. She vowed to have the last laugh.

She marched over to the officials. "That is a mad cow. I want her shot immediately."

Bellowing and shaking her head, Henrietta blew bubbles everywhere.

Matt Farmer came down out of the stands. "Now wait just a minute. There was nothing wrong with this cow this morning. I insist on having a vet check her over before any decision is made."

He picked up the piece of rope dangling from her halter and led her to the fence and tied her up. Then he took a good look at the foam around Henrietta's muzzle. It was soapsuds.

"Look, everyone. It's soapsuds. Someone gave this cow soapsuds to drink. Who would do that?"

Mrs. Leadbottom grabbed her daughter by the ear and asked, "Did you do it, Angela?"

Angela admitted the truth.

Mrs. Leadbottom shook her daughter and said, "You apologize to Mr. Farmer and Susie."

Angela whined, "But you wanted me to win."

Mrs. Leadbottom shook her again.

By this time, Angela was in tears. Through her tears, in a quivering voice, she said, "I'm sorry."

Mr. Farmer carried four buckets of clean water to Henrietta. The bubbles gradually disappeared. The mad cow disease had been diagnosed and treated successfully.

During the mature cow show, the judge named Henrietta the grand champion cow. For the first time in history, the grand champion cow was clean on both the inside and the outside.

The End

ONIONS CAN MAKE A GROWN MAN CRY

Mr. Farmer spooned sugar into his coffee, then added milk. He stirred the mixture, picked up the cup, and slowly sipped the hot liquid.

Eagerly, he picked up the latest *Hoard's Dairyman* magazine while he drank his coffee. Suddenly, he looked at Mrs. Farmer. "I've been reading about intensive grazing in the farm magazines."

"Intensive grazing?"

"Yes, intensive grazing. We pastured the cows years ago until we got high-tech and confined them to the barn and feed lot."

"How is this different from what we used to do?"

"First of all, we have to pick out the area we will use for grazing. If the field already grows alfalfa and grass, so much the better. If not, I may have to seed more grass. After that, I put a good fence around the whole field; then divide the field into small pastures with electric fence. Every day or so we move the fence and the herd to a new section of pasture. When the cows go on a new section, the area they've already eaten has a chance to grow again. It's supposed to work out great and save us labor and money in the long run."

Mrs. Farmer stared at Mr. Farmer in disbelief, "Are you sure you know what you are doing, Matt Farmer? Those ornery critters of yours will get out."

Mr. Farmer snorted, "Not if I build the fence correctly."

Hands on her hips, Mrs. Farmer replied, "I'm warning you, Mr. Farmer, if those cows of yours trample my garden, you'll answer to me."

Mr. Farmer kissed his wife's cheek and patted her shoulder, affectionately. "Don't worry, dear. Everything will work out fine."

Mr. Farmer spent the next few days stringing an electric fence around the field he intended to use for his pasture.

The day the fence was finished, Mr. Farmer walked into the barn. "Hello ladies, have I got a surprise for you! I'm not going to feed you anymore. You're going to go out to the new pasture and feed yourselves."

The cows babbled at once. Hazel, the red and white Holstein, was particularly vocal. "I like my hay and grain, Mr. Farmer. I don't want to try something new."

"Nevertheless, ladies, you are going to pasture, that's final."

As soon as the cows were in the pasture, they kicked up their heels and ran like frolicking calves, tails flying like flags in the wind.

Matt Farmer called, "Hey, you cows, stop that running. You'll be giving buttermilk tonight."

Everything went fine for a few days, but then the weather turned hot.

One ninety-five degree day, Hazel said to the other cows, "I'm tired of hard work in all of this heat."

Henrietta, a black and white Holstein said, "There's too many bugs out here too. I can't swish my tail fast enough to keep them off me."

Hildegarde, the Brown Swiss cow chimed in, "I think I know a way we could get back in the nice shady barn and let Mr. Farmer feed us like he used to."

Hazel and Henrietta put their heads close to Hildegarde's.

Hazel asked, "What can we do?"

"I bet if we got out and ate Mrs. Farmer's garden, she would insist Mr. Farmer put us back in the nice shady barn," said Hildegarde.

Hazel did a little tap dance. " O-o-o-h, you have a devious mind, Hildegarde. What a great idea."

Henrietta sighed. "We can't get out of this fence. It's built too good."

Hildegarde snorted. "Where's your spirit of adventure? One of us has to go through the fence and break it."

Henrietta sighed, "Not me. I don't like touching that electric stuff. It stings."

Hazel said, "I've got an idea." She got down on her knees, stretched her neck under the wire, and wriggled like a snake under the wire.

Henrietta was too tall. She sighed. "I'll never make it."

Suddenly, she had an idea. She stepped back a few feet, got a running start, and sailed over the fence.

Hazel and Henrietta started toward Mrs. Farmer's garden.

Hildegarde mooed, "Hey, wait for me." She wasn't one to be left behind.

She stepped twice as far back as Henrietta had and charged through the fence. Insulators and fence posts flew in every direction.

The rest of the herd followed her to Mrs. Farmer's garden. They tasted everything in sight, but especially the onions. Oh, they were good.

About that time, Mr. and Mrs. Farmer discovered the cows and chased them to the barn.

Of course, when Mr. Farmer milked the cows that night the milk tasted and smelled like onions. Mr. Farmer had to dump it all down the drain. His profit for the day was down the drain, just like the milk.

The moral of the story is: Be careful! Onions can make even a grown man cry.

The End

THE RACE

The race was underway. Missy, excited, paced herself well. She checked her watch – right on schedule at the mile marker. She glanced at her friend Susan, smiled, and gave her an OK sign. Hard work and practice were paying off. They were ahead of the pack.

Missy looked ahead and frowned. What was the matter with the runner in front of her? She thought he stumbled. When she looked again, she saw him clutching his chest, as if in pain. She looked around, nobody noticed him. If she helped him, she would lose the race. She bit her lip. Were people blind? No one else noticed him? Darn it!

She recognized the man – it was Mr. Barnett, the teacher. The same Mr. Barnett who had tortured her all year. Just last week he had humiliated her in algebra class.

A zillion thoughts flashed through her head in the next few seconds. Stopping to help him would waste the training for the race... She would have to wait a whole year for the next Lake-stride half-marathon... Could she help a man who had been so mean to her? It would serve him right if he suffered... But what if he died?

Knowing she could never let even her worst enemy die, she stopped to administer CPR.

Race officials finally saw what was going on and took over for her. She continued the race and had to settle for sixth place.

Later, when the awards were handed out, they honored her with a plaque saying, "FOR PUTTING PEOPLE FIRST, YOU ARE A WINNER."

The End

MARSILLA

"Hello, boys and girls, my name is Marsilla. My whole name is Miracle Acres Marsilla.

I'm a calf, and not just any ordinary calf, I'm a Brown Swiss calf.

I was born one frosty May morning. My mother licked my coat until it was dry.

When a cow licks her calf, that calf knows how much her mother loves her.

But love isn't the only reason a cow licks her calf. Licking helps the calf's circulation increase. It's heart starts beating, strongly. It's lungs fill with air.

When I was born, my hair was nearly white. Over the months, it gradually turned darker. Now it's a rich chocolate brown color.

Some calves are born, live, and die on the same farm, but not me. I was born on a big dairy farm in Wisconsin. One day, a boy named Dan visited the farm with his father. The father bought two cows. Dan fell in love with me. He begged my owners to sell me to him. They did.

I rode with two big cows all the way from the middle of Wisconsin. We went around Chicago and all the way up the west side of Michigan to a dairy farm north of Scottville. I can't tell you how scared I was. I shivered and shook.

I mooed a lot. I said, "Ma! Ma!" over and over.

At the new farm, Dan petted me a lot. He fed me milk replacer, calf pellets, and hay. I grew a little bit every day

Dan put a halter on me and taught me to follow him. At first, I kicked up my heels and ran around and around. It was fun. But then I learned to follow Dan wherever he led me. I stopped when he wanted me to and walked when he wanted me to. I was a good calf. Dan gave me a shampoo and a bath. He combed my hair until it shone. He even washed inside my ears with a soft cloth. Then he took me to the county fair.

At the fair, people walked through the barns looking at all the animals. They always stopped to pet me. They thought I was pretty because I was different from all the black and white Holstein calves. I won a purple junior ribbon because I'm so beautiful.

After the fair ended, Dan took me home. He turned me loose in the pasture. I kicked up my heels, lifted my tail in the air, and ran, happy to be home again.

By the time I am two years old, I'll be a full grown cow. All cows' milk is very healthy for growing boys and girls. But Brown Swiss milk has more protein and more solids than ordinary milk. Take my word for it. Brown Swiss milk tastes yummy."

The End

THE WIMP

Harvey's left hand stretched the left side of his face. His right had swiped the taut skin with a sharp razor.

"Harv-e-e."

Sylvia's shrill voice floated up the stairs. "Better hurry. You'll be late. Harve-e. You'll be late. Harve-e. Answer me. Are you getting ready for work?"

"Yes, dear." Harvey groaned, muttering to himself, "What else would I be doing this time of morning?"

He hated his wife's voice in the morning. Nagging, nagging, nagging. When had she turned from a loving sex kitten to an absolute shrew? For that matter, when had he evolved from his own man to a wimp? Sylvia, the captain? He, the crew? Harvey considered options. He could walk out and never return, but it was against his nature to treat anybody that way. And he and Sylvia had been close at one time. Very close. So close they'd produced two little dependents. He couldn't bear to leave those kids. He loved them, dearly.

One or two other ideas formed in the back of his mind. Blood? Damn! He'd cut himself. Better concentrate on shaving now and make decisions later. Harvey shaved the lather off, sluiced water on his face, then wiped it on the towel.

Harvey stared at his image, turning left and then right. A pretty ordinary looking face, except for the blood. Not too fat. Not too thin. Not too handsome. Nice brown eyes. His dark brows had a nice arch to them, emphasized by a full head of dark brown hair. Nose, neither too large nor too small.

Maybe his mouth should be firmer. Yes, definitely, it should be firmer. He tried a few facial expressions. A stern look. A smile. Lastly, he tried looking mad. He sighed.

A myriad of sounds drifted up from downstairs.

Two-year old Danny yelling at the top of his lungs. "I want Pops. Pops. Pops."

Billy, banged on his high chair tray with a spoon, accompanying his drumming with "Da-da-da-goo-goo."

In the background a rock song blared. Harvey pictured Sylvia swinging her hips in time to the music. She did have nice hips. That part of her anatomy had been one of the first things he'd noticed about her. He frowned. Sylvia. He wondered if his in-laws had named her a feminine name like Elizabeth or Emily, if she'd be so bossy. He needed a solution to this unhappy rut before he was in so deep, he was buried alive.

He picked up his shirt, slipped his arms into it, and headed for the kitchen, buttoning the last button on his sleeve as he walked through the kitchen door.

"Hurry up, Harvey. My goodness, it's taking you forever this morning."

Harvey looked at his watch. "I'm right on schedule."

Bacon sizzled in the frying pan. Two pieces of toast popped up in the toaster.

"Sit down, Harvey. Eat your breakfast. Here, hold the baby while you eat." Not waiting for an answer, she thrust their six-month old son onto his lap.

"Sylvia, can't he sit in the high chair? He'll have his sticky hands all over my shirt and tie."

"Billy likes to sit on your lap. He'll be too fussy in the high chair. I can't stand to hear him whine this early in the morning. Here's your eggs and toast. Hurry. Eat." Sylvia giggled. "Oh Billy, don't stick your hands in Daddy's eggs."

Harvey grabbed a napkin and wiped his son's hands. Just once he'd like to wear a shirt to work minus baby handprints.

"Here's a list of things for you to do after work." Sylvia handed him a slip of paper. "Go to the cleaners; pick up my dress. Stop at the store; buy milk, bread, and baby cereal. And don't waste time about it. You have to mow the lawn when you get home tonight."

"Yes, dear."

"It's time for you to leave now, Harvey. Here, give me the baby."

He slipped his arm into his jacket. He sidled up to his wife and aimed a kiss at her mouth, but she neatly turned her head, so it landed on the side of her face.

Sighing, Harvey stopped with his hand on the doorknob. "By the way, Sylvia, I have to attend some classes at the college every night this week. You'll have to do your own errands."

"Every night?" Sylvia's face fell. "Why didn't you say something before this? Why wait until Monday morning to tell me? I have so many things planned for you to do during the evenings this week."

"Sorry... I... uh... I forgot. You'll either have to do stuff yourself, or wait until I get a chance to do it,"

Sylvia pouted. "Well, that ruins all my plans and schedules."

•   •   •

It was nearly eleven when Harvey walked into the house Friday night. Sylvia sat in a chair in the living room, facing the television. Hearing his footsteps, she looked up with a look of genuine relief on her face. Sylvia's lips curved into a tentative half smile.

What had she thought? Had she thought he might leave? She seemed pleased he was home.

Harvey carried a large letter-size envelope. He opened it and pulled out a thick piece of paper, handing it to Sylvia.

Sylvia took it into her hands and moved closer to the lamp. She read it once, started at the top and read it again.

At Sylvia's reaction, Harvey stared in amazement. She giggled hysterically. Collapsing into a chair, she rolled back and forth, laughing until tears rolled down her cheeks.

Fifteen minutes passed before she could speak coherently.

Sylvia stood up and said, "Oh, Harvey, a certificate for Assertiveness Training. How funny. I've been trying to make you assert yourself for years. I didn't think you would ever do it."

Standing proud and tall, Harvey stared awkwardly into Sylvia's blue eyes. "Well, dear wife, you won't push me around anymore."

Sylvia wiped a tear from her right eye, and apprehensive expression on her face. "You're not leaving me, are you Harvey?"

"No, sweetheart, I love you. Decisions about when and where I do things from now on will be up to me."

Sylvia threw her arms around his neck. "Oh, honey I love you too."

Harvey hugged her tightly, "We'd better go to bed, woman. I want to get up early in the morning and mow the lawn."

The End

CHIP OFF THE OLD BLOCK

Marie rubbed Chuck's shoulder and shook him fiercely.

From far away, he heard her voice, "Chuck. Come on, Chuck, wake up."

She pummeled his back.

Chuck surfaced slowly from a deep sleep. He raised up on one elbow. "Huh, what?" He rubbed his eyes and tried to focus on his wife's face in the dark bedroom. "What's the matter?"

In a quavering voice she said, "I'm worried. It's four in the morning and Billy's not home yet."

Chuck groaned. "Good grief! Is that what you woke me for? Why, for Pete's sake? What can I do until he gets home? Or the police call saying he's been in an accident? Answer me that. Just what do you expect me to do?"

In a meek little voice, Marie whispered, "I just thought you would want to know. He's your son, too. Your pride and joy. A chip off the old block." She rolled over and turned her back on him.

Chuck laid there in the dark. Wide awake. Shadows and reflections of light sped along the wall whenever a car came down the road. Each time he expected the car to turn into their driveway, but it zipped on by. Darn kid. What was the matter with him? Didn't he think they would worry about him? No good came from staying out so late. What in the world could a teen-ager do after midnight that he couldn't do before?

Beside him, Marie began to snore, lightly.

"Great. Just Hunky Dory. She wakes me up; then falls asleep herself," Chuck fumed silently, mad at both his wife and son.

By five a.m., he crawled out of bed. He looked out the window at the space he usually parked his car. The mercury yard light shone on the bare ground. Empty. The space was empty.

"Darn kid." He muttered under his breath before he shuffled, bare-foot, down the stairs.

In the kitchen, he made a pot of coffee. At five-thirty, he poured a second cup of coffee and sat at the table, reading the *National Geographic*.

A car drove in the driveway. Seconds later, the back door opened. The guilty look on his son's face almost cracked Chuck up, but he managed to keep his own expression stern and straight. A parent has to keep an upper hand.

Sheepishly, Bill said, "Hi, Dad. What are you doing up so early?"

"What do you think?" He slowly got to his feet. He knew he intimidated his son when he towered above him. "Waiting for you. You went to a basketball game at seven last night." He pointed at the time on the microwave's digital figures. "Look at the time. Where have you been anyway?"

Bill shuffled his feet, all the while jiggling the keys in his pocket. He shrugged. He picked up a magazine and flipped through the pages. "A bunch of us were over at Mike's house watching videos."

Gruffly, Chuck asked, "Didn't you ever hear of a phone? You know, that invention by Alexander Graham Bell?" He pointed to the telephone on the wall. "I pay plenty each month so my son can let his mother and I know where he is and when he'll be late."

Bill shrugged, defiantly. "You guys wouldn't hear it, if you were sleeping. You never hear it from your room." He raised one shoulder. "I knew where I was."

"That's not good enough. Your mother was worried sick. I want to know where you are, especially when you are driving my car." Chuck walked purposefully toward his son. "Give me the keys." He extended his hand.

Bill dropped the keys into his father's outstretched hand.

Chuck stuffed them in the front pocket of his jeans. "Sorry, son. You're grounded for the next month."

"What? Dad? For crying out loud, Dad." Bill slammed the magazine down on the table. "I'll be eighteen years old soon. I'll graduate in a couple of months. I've got an important party to attend next Saturday night." He glared at his father.

Hands on his hips, Chuck glared back. "Too bad, you should have thought of that sooner, young man. While you're in my house, you'll follow my rules. Stand here and argue about it, I'll make it twice as long. How about two months?"

Bill headed toward the stairway.

"Where are you going?"

"Bed."

"Oh, no. No, you're not." Chuck pointed to the outside door. "Get out to the barn and feed the cows, young man. If you can stay out all night, you can work all day. You'll be tired enough to go to bed at a decent hour tonight."

•　　　　•　　　　•

Later in the week, Chuck ran into a buddy from his own school days.

He shook hands with his former classmate. "Jerry, how are you?"

"How ya doing, Chuck?"

After a few minutes of small talk, Jerry slapped Chuck on the back. "Hey, remember some of those parties we had back in the old days?"

He chuckled. "When we were seniors, we had parties every Saturday night."

Chuck laughed. "Yeah. I was really lucky to get home in time to do the milking some Sunday mornings. My Dad had a fit, especially when I drove his car." Suddenly, the similarity of his situation and his son's hit him. "Oh, oh," he muttered under his breath.

Puzzled, Jerry said, "What's matter, buddy?"

Sheepishly, Chuck ran his hand through his hair. "I just grounded my son last week for doing the same thing."

Jerry chortled and slapped Chuck on the back. "A chip off the old block, eh?"

Chuck frowned. Absent–mindedly, he said good-bye to his old friend and continued down the street, deep in thought. He remembered those Saturday nights twenty-five years ago.

Later that evening while he and Bill milked cows together, Chuck said, "You know son, I met an old friend from high school today."

Bill shrugged, "So?"

"Jerry reminded me about my own senior high school days. My friends and I held parties every weekend. I stayed out all night with my dad's car. He was furious. I couldn't understand why."

Bill stood still.

Chuck sensed, instead of saw, his son holding his breath. He continued, "I may have made a mistake when I grounded you. I've decided I'll return your privileges, if you promise to let us know where you are and when you'll be late. Parents can't help but worry."

Bill's face lit up. "Okay Dad." He grinned and gave his father a thumbs up sign. "It's a deal."

Chuck watched his son saunter away, a slight strut to his gait. "Yes sir, that boy is a chip off the old block."

The End

ALBERTA CLIPPER

Mike stirred. What a dream! Real sexual longing throbbed through his body. Longing for Angela Bradbury. Now, wide awake, he envisioned voluptuous breasts encased in a seductive black lace-nightgown. Had he dreamt of Angela? She had been coming on to him for weeks, flirting, inviting him to visit her apartment. Capitulation seemed inevitable.

The furious wind howled. It rattled the windows, shook the rafters. The floors creaked. Mike listened. If this kept up, driving to work would be impossible.

The alarm shrilled. Mike stumbled across the room, silenced the instrument. He parted the drapes, stared out the window. The wind shrieked. Snow blew across the yard, horizontally.

Mike flipped the radio switch.

The announcer said, "An Alberta Clipper has blustered into the area. There is zero visibility. White-outs. All schools are cancelled. The state police have ordered all motorists off the roads. Do not attempt travel without permission. If you do, you will be arrested."

Carolyn snuggled under the covers. "Great. You can't work today. Let's take advantage of the opportunity" she invited, softly. "Come back to bed."

Mike froze. They hadn't made love in months. Make love to frumpy Carolyn in her ripped flannel nightgown after dreaming of sensual, wanton Angela? Now she wanted to?

"Um... I have to go to the bathroom. Guess I'll stay up. I have some reading I want to do."

"Suit yourself," she mumbled, "I'm staying in bed for a while." Disappointed, she remembered earlier days in their marriage, he would have jumped her bones in a minute back then.

Mike shivered, tugging on cold jeans, and slipped a sweatshirt over his head. He went to the kitchen in need of a caffeine-fix. The water trickled through the grounds a drop at a time. Impatiently, he leafed through the pages of a magazine he wanted to read. Concentration was impossible.

Stuck home with Carolyn? What would they do? They had nothing in common except for the kids, of course. Tonight was the night.

It was Carolyn's fault. Mike remembered how his mother, God rest her soul, no matter how busy, changed into a clean dress, combed her hair, and put on makeup before his father came home from work. When they asked why, she always replied, "To look nice for your father, of course."

Carolyn didn't dress up for him. She wore faded sweatshirts and faded blue jeans day after day. No makeup. Tousled, uncombed hair completed the picture. Nose in a book, she ignored him or pounded away on the typewriter night after night. What did she expect him to do anyway?

After breakfast, Mike wandered into the living room. He admitted to himself, Carolyn is a good cook. The kids followed him.

Jimmy said, "Play a game with us, Dad."

Elizabeth argued, "No, let's put a puzzle together. That's what we always do during storms." She ran to the cupboard and picked up a puzzle. She turned around, appealed to Mike. "You'll help us, won't you Dad?"

Mike couldn't resist his daughter's baby blue eyes. "We'll do the puzzle first." He put his arm around his son's shoulders. "Then we'll play games. We've got all day."

Occupying myself, with the kids will keep me from thinking about Angela. This will be a long day. I just know it.

In the kitchen, Carolyn washed the dishes by hand. A few days ago the dishwasher had gone on the blink. Calling a repairman was expensive. She bought Jimmy shoes last week. The week before she paid the car insurance, good grief, always something. Maybe she should look for a job. She added checking the want ads to her agenda.

Brrr, the wind seeped through the walls. Homemade soup simmered on the stove. It was a good day to bake. She lit the oven; mixed a batch of bread. While the bread rose, she made cookies and baked them.

She brooded about how far apart she and Mike had become. She tried to remember the last time they had made love. A dismal failure. It had been Halloween. Now it was February.

The whole scene played before her eyes in slow motion. She had had a bad cold. Mike wanted to make love. Every time he kissed her, she couldn't breathe and pulled away, gasping and coughing. Mike had been disgusted.

She suggested they make love without the kissing. He said he couldn't do that. He rolled over and went to sleep. For two or three nights, she had been so sick she hadn't cared. But after she was well again, he still ignored her.

He rolled over and slept night after night; not even kissing her good night.

Carolyn borrowed paperback romance novels from the library to escape her troubles. After reading three a day for a month, she decided she could write novels better than the ones she read. She typed long after Mike fell asleep every night.

Eventually, she realized how long it had been since they made love. It was her fault, she knew it. She stayed up too late. She began going to bed before Mike. A lot of good that did her. He backed into bed, keeping his back to her, and fell asleep every night. After a week of that treatment, she bought a bottle of wine, pouring him a glass of wine before bedtime. Wine always turned her on but didn't seem to affect Mike one bit. It was a funny thing. The more he ignored her; the more her desire increased. Frustrated, she wondered why people always want what they can't have.

Carolyn reached the end of her rope. Their marriage was in serious jeopardy; she just knew it. What if Mike had a girlfriend? Why did he stay so late at the office several nights a week? For the past week she had been mentally rehearsing speeches... Mike, we have to talk. Mike, do you love me? Mike, don't you love me anymore? Mike, I need to make love to you...

During her troubled thought process, Carolyn wiped off the table, cleaned the stove and swept the floor. She thought, because of the storm, Mike can't leave... Maybe this is my last chance to hash things out with him. I have to talk with him.

What would she do if he wanted a divorce? She had needs too. She looked down at her body, middle-aged and dumpy just about described it. No wonder Mike wasn't turned on. If he left her, what would she do about sex? How would she meet another man? If she didn't have Mike, would she go to bars by herself?

Carolyn sliced the freshly baked bread, took paper plates, knives, and butter into the living room to Mike and the kids. She was surprised to see they didn't even have the television on.

Jimmy and Elizabeth clamored for her to help them.

Carolyn reached over and found a couple of pieces, but said, "I'm all dirty from baking. I'm going to clean up, I'll help later, after I've had a shower and changed my clothes."

In the bathroom, Carolyn carefully shaved her legs and underarms. After her shower, she generously fluffed bath powder over her body. She decided a sexy, red nightgown she had purchased in a moment of insanity then saved for a special occasion. She covered the nightgown with a matching negligee. A frantic last ditch effort made her spray cologne on strategic spots. Hopefully, Mike would notice.

During the day, working on the puzzle with the kids, Mike had begun to realize how much the kids meant to his life. Elizabeth with her blue eyes, blonde hair, and slender body had a bubbly personality. While Jimmy had dark hair, brown eyes, and a sturdy boy's body. The family comic, he always made jokes about something. Watching his children, Mike realized he couldn't leave them for a fling with a blonde from the typing pool. What had he been thinking?

Carolyn entered the room with mugs of hot chocolate laced with marshmallows for the four of them.

Jimmy and Elizabeth chorused, "Can you help us with the puzzle now, Mom?"

Carolyn grinned. "I certainly can. I have the kitchen and myself all cleaned up."

Mike sat in his easy chair. The card table was set up in front of him.

The kids had pulled folding chairs up to the table for themselves. Carolyn perched on the right arm of Mike's chair. She looked over the puzzle pieces. The one she wanted was way to Mike's left. She reached in front of him, making sure her breast brushed against his arm. She chose those pieces on that side of the table several times. Once, she had to slide her left arm around his neck when she lost her balance.

Mike inhaled Carolyn's perfume. She smelled super good. When she brushed against him, his desire awakened. He looked at his watch, "It's time for you kids to go to bed."

"Aw, Dad," they both pleaded. "We won't have school tomorrow. Even if it stops snowing, the roads won't be plowed. Can't we stay up a little longer?"

Mike glanced at Carolyn. "What do you think?"

Carolyn, anxious to have a heart-to-heart talk with Mike, knew they had to get their feelings out in the open. They had to discuss their marriage or it wouldn't be a marriage much longer. She certainly knew she couldn't go on as they had the last four months.

She said firmly, "You can stay up another half hour. After that it's bedtime, like it or not."

After she had kissed the kids goodnight and tucked them in bed, Carolyn detoured to the kitchen and returned with a bottle of Chablis and two glasses. She poured wine into each glass. Handed him one and settled on the arm of his chair with the other one.

"You smell so good. How about us going to bed too?"

After all the soul-searching today, Carolyn knew they needed to discuss their marriage, if it was going to survive. She thought they called using alcohol "Dutch courage". He set her glass on the table, trying to ignore Mike's hand around her waist; his fingers creeping closer and closer to her breast.

"I think we have to talk about our marriage."

He kissed the side of her neck. "What about our marriage, hmm?"

She bit her lip, took a deep breath, and spoke. "For months now, you've turned your back on me in bed. I can't stand it anymore. I have needs too. Physical needs. Don't you love me anymore? She couldn't help it. She planned to be cool, calm, and collected, but emotions got the best of her. Tears rolled down her cheeks.

"Honey, I can't explain what's been going on. Mid-life crisis, I guess." He cuddled her to him. "I'm almost forty. Life seemed to be passing me by. You didn't seem to give me the same respect my mother gave my father. I know you're not like my mother. You're you. I thought we had grown too far apart. I didn't think we had anything in common anymore. Today, I know how much I love you and the kids." He kissed her long and hard, a searing kiss that took her breath away. "The storm raged around the house today. It made the house a cozy nest. A nest I never want to leave."

Carolyn responded to his ardent kisses with kisses of her own. In unison, arm in arm, they moved to the bedroom for the most incredible lovemaking either had ever experienced.

The next morning, they looked out on a clean white world. They had weathered the storm. The sun shone brightly. A new day. A renewed marriage. Better than any romance novel Carolyn had ever read.

The End

TORNADO

The wind whipped the restaurant door; it slammed shut behind the two women. Laughing, they shook raindrops from their coats. Susan's dark hair; wet from rain, glistened in the light.

She said, "Wow! What a storm!" She stomped her feet, shaking excess water from her shoes.

Water soaked, Jennie's blonde hair appeared shades darker. She looked through the large front window at the front of the restaurant. "We escaped the weather just in time. Good grief! Look at that rain sheet across the street."

The rain sounded like hail, it hit the window so hard.

The hostess appeared and led them to a table next to a window. She handed them menus, telling them their waitress would be with them in few minutes.

The storm intensified as the women watched. The sky darkened. The wind whipped everything in its path. Papers, hats, and loose debris of all sorts flew by. The waitress appeared carrying a coffee pot. At their request, she poured coffee before taking their orders. Susan ordered the chicken salad and Jennie a fruit salad.

Jennie commented, "There goes our shopping spree. There's nothing I need bad enough to shop in this weather."

"Now we have a good excuse to sit here and pig out." Susan laughed at her own joke. She sipped from her cup. "Hmmm, this hot coffee hits the spot."

The waitress delivered their salads. They eagerly attacked them. They continued to monitor the storm as they ate and talked, not necessarily in that order. Jennie and Susan had been friends almost their whole lives, so they were seldom at a loss for words. Their conversation drifted back to when they first met their husbands, Jim and Mike. They laughed at how "the boys," as they called them, tried to "rescue" them the night they first met, when Susan's old car had broken down and left the two friends standing along the side of the road. Jim and Mike had pulled up to help the ladies and neither young man was very familiar with the differences between a wrench or screwdriver.

"Oh, my God." Susan dropped her fork and stood in one motion.

Jennie followed Susan's terror-stricken gaze. A funnel cloud, dark, wide, and angry was headed straight toward them. A tornado.

"Quick, under the table." Without waiting to see what her friend did, she slid under the table and buried her head under her arms.

Susan stood, fascinated by the storm, frozen in place. She watched a power pole snap in two and crash to the street, sparks flying. The wind sounded like a freight train rumbling through town. The furious storm picked up a white Cadillac coming down the street and tossed it end for end. Susan screamed as the car crashed through the window, landing a few feet away from the table Jennie crouched under. That was close enough for Susan. She dove under another table near by.

The whole building shook. Bricks, lumber, and glass tumbled into a pile of rubble. A portion of the roof caved in. Restaurant patrons screamed and cried in terror. Then an eerie silence prevailed for a minute as the storm deserted the devastation it had created only minutes before.

Sirens, heard in the distance, became louder as the fire department arrived on the scene. Rescuers surveyed the damage and organized the workers.

The deep male voice of the fire chief shouted, "People, if you can hear me, let us know where you are so we can dig you out."

Susan thought about Mike and the kids. What would they do if she didn't make it? Jim and Mike were just settling into the afternoon baseball game on television. They had had a good soccer practice with the kids, picked up a quick lunch for them at McDonald's and sent them upstairs to play.

Mike said this was close is as they've come to a boys' night out in ages. He was kidding, of course.

A special news bulletin came on the screen, "Ladies and gentlemen, we interrupt this program to inform you that several buildings have collapsed. We suspect several people may be buried in the rubble. The fire department and rescue squads are on the scene. Please avoid the downtown area and give them room to work. We'll keep you posted."

At the same time, both men said, "The girls are downtown."

"Yeah. They were going to lunch at that restaurant they like right on the main drag. After lunch they were going shopping."

They both moved to get their jackets.

Mike said, "I'd better tell the kids where we are going." He moved to the stairs and yelled, "Kids, Jim and I are going downtown a minute. We'll be back as soon as we can."

Twelve year old Mandy appeared at the top of the stairs, a concerned expression on her face. "You think Mommy was in that tornado, don't you?"

"I think it's a good possibility."

Her face lined with worry, she asked, "Can Timmy and I go?"

She looked wistful and scared. But he thought he and Jim might have to walk hard and fast to get near enough to see what was going on.

"I think you'd better stay here, honey. We might have to park and walk a long way. Please pray for Mommy and Jennie."

"OK, Daddy."

She looked so sad when she turned to go back to her room that Mike almost relented. But he knew he was right to leave the kids at home.

Hunched over the wheel, Mike peered through the rain. Streets, traffic lights, and signs all hid behind the sheeting rain. Basically, the streets were deserted. A few cars headed in the same direction they did. Three blocks away from their destination, the police had blocked off the street. A police officer motioned, blew his whistle and tried to stop them. Mike and Jim told him their wives were in the restaurant. They were going, come hell or high water.

Debris littered the ground everywhere. They stepped over pieces of wood, bricks, garbage, metal, and glass. Shocked, they stared at the devastation and activity when they reached the street where the restaurant was located. Fire trucks and rescue squad trucks were parked everywhere. Fireman ran from the building and back to the trucks.

One of them yelled at Mike and Jim, "Hey, where do you guys think you're going?"

"We're pretty sure our wives are in the restaurant," they answered in unison.

Meanwhile, Susan managed to make sounds loud enough to be heard by rescue people. They began digging to reach her. Jennie saw a car fender and knew a car was buried next to her. She smelled gasoline. The odor nauseated her. The smell must be coming from that car.

She coughed. "Help me. Someone. help me."

Jim heard her cry. "Hey, you guys, help me quick. My wife is under here. Help me." He dug with his hands, throwing boards and bricks out of the way.

A few feet away, helping hands pulled Susan from the wreckage. She was conscious and trying to convince rescuers she was fine. Even so, they insisted on sending her to the hospital.

Mike wanted to go with Susan, but he knew Jim needed help. "I'll help Jim and then come to the hospital, sweetheart," he promised.

Heat from the fire singed Jim's eyebrows and arms. "Hey, you guys, we've got to get this fire out. My wife is under here."

Firemen moved in and poured water on the flames.

Mike lifted a large piece of wood off Jenny's legs. Mike and Jim picked up the lifesaving table. They pulled more wet debris off her before Jim held her tightly in his arms.

"Jennie, are you alright?"

Jennie coughed. "I... I think I'll be better if you don't break my ribs."

She still had her sense of humor. Jim thanked God for that as they loaded her into the ambulance.

At the hospital, Jim and Mike flipped through uninteresting magazines in the emergency waiting room.

Mike stood up and paced around the room. "That was a dumb conversation I started this afternoon."

Jim knew exactly which conversation he meant. He said, "I know exactly which conversation you mean."

"I can't believe we even talked about that kind of stuff. I'll never forget today. From now on, I'll appreciate Jennie."

Mike agreed. "I'll never take Susan for granted again. We both came close to losing something precious today."

The End

ACCIDENTS WILL HAPPEN

Quickly, the two women jumped from the dark blue Dodge shadow. Mary Lee pulled the keys from the ignition and grabbed her cellphone in one motion. They rushed down the ravine to the overturned dirty red pickup.

Mary Lee turned to her friend. "It looks bad. I'm scared to see what's in that truck."

Susan answered, "Me too. But we have to do it. There's no one else. Whoever is in that truck needs us."

Seconds ago, horrified, Mary Lee slammed on the brakes as they witnessed the driver ahead of them go off the left side of the freeway, over-correct, and then go off the right side of the freeway, over-correct, and careen down the embankment, rolling over as it went.

Now, minutes later, the wheels still spun in wild abandon. The driver's head hung at an odd angle. Perhaps he was unconscious.

Always one with the smart remark, Susan quipped, "Don't light a cigarette, we'll all go up in smoke."

Mary Lee rolled her eyes and gave Susan a 'get serious' look. She punched 911 on her cell phone.

"There's a pickup overturned on U.S. 31 south of Ludington. Send the sheriff, a rescue squad, and an ambulance. Right away. Hurry."

Mary Lee had to answer so many questions from the dispatcher such as her name, phone number, where she lived.

When she hung up, she muttered to Susan, "What the heck difference does it make what my name is or where I live? We just witnessed an accident and called for help. I had to give that woman my whole life's history."

"Calm down, Mary Lee. They just want to be sure you're not a crackpot making a crank call." Susan bent down and looked at the driver. "Should we try to get him out or wait until help gets here?"

Mary Lee squatted and looked at the driver through the window. She frowned. "He looks pretty big. We probably can't handle him. What if we dropped him? He could sue us. It happens all the time. You're always reading about these kinds of things in the paper. A good Samaritan stops to help an accident victim and gets her pants sued off or loses her shirt."

Susan peered at him through the window. "I feel so sorry for him, hanging like there like that."

"He's unconscious. He can't feel a thing." Always on the lookout for a good-looking man, Mary Lee bent down and looked at him again. "My, he certainly is handsome, isn't he?"

Just as man-crazy, Susan agreed. "Dark curly hair, strong jaw. Nice straight nose, yep, they sure add up to one handsome fellow."

Just then, incredible blue eyes opened and looked straight into Susan's soft gray ones. Her heart skipped a beat; then thudded loudly.

Embarrassed to be caught staring at him, she said to him, "Don't worry, help is on the way." She turned to Mary Lee, "Do you smell smoke?"

Mary Lee sniffed, "No, but I have a cold. Do you?"

Susan sniffed again. "Yes, yes, I do."

The guy in the truck knocked on the window. "Get me out of here. There's a fire in here."

Flames began under the dash and were licking at his feet. The women saw them now. Susan struggled to open the driver's door. It wouldn't budge. Mary Lee threw her cellphone halfway up the hill and ran to the other side. That door wouldn't open either.

"Break the window. Hurry."

Susan found a piece of two by four that had fallen from his truck. She grabbed it.

"Shut your eyes," she commanded the man.

She rammed the window once, twice, three times. It shattered into smithereens, sending a shower of glass in every direction.

The man undid his seatbelt and tried to crawl through the window. "I think my leg is broken," He told them. "I can't move it."

The women each pulled on an arm. With his help, they managed to get him out of the truck and onto the grass. The fire burned rapidly now with flames visible.

Susan said, "Smell that gas. We better get further away from here before that truck blows up."

She and Mary Lee pulled the man, dragging him until their arms ached.

Finally, when they could not go another inch, they sat on the ground, panting.

An explosion rocked the earth. Flames shot high in the sky. Sirens screamed above the roar of the fire.

Susan said, "Now they show up."

"Better late than never, they always say." Mary Lee motioned to the ambulance crew. "This man is hurt. He was in that truck."

"Good thing for him you girls were here. You're kind of like the police in the back ground doing the work with no one noticing," said an EMT.

"I guess you're right. We're unsung heroes."

"Well, this unsung hero is going to go home and take a shower."

Later that afternoon, Mary Lee bumped into Susan in the hospital gift shop. Susan was wearing a tight blue dress, one of her favorites. Mary Lee was similarly dressed. Both women held books in their hands, as they peered at the other's purchases; they realized they had the same idea in mind. With her usual quick wit, Susan asked Mary Lee if she would like to ride up in the elevator with her.

As they neared the hospital room of the man they worked so hard to rescue earlier in the day, they heard voices coming from the doorway. Susan quietly knocked on the door and was quickly acknowledged. As the two friends entered the hospital room, they were surprised to see a beautiful blonde woman standing alongside the bed.

John said "Hello girls! I'd like you to meet my wife."

The End